THE MILITARY CHILD CHRONICLES

Written by
Athens E. Pellegrino

Illustrated by
Cody Taylor

To our brave military families.
Thank you

ISBN 978-1-7365126-0-9

Layout design by Ryan Durnford, edited by Brooke Vitale

Once upon a time, there was a brave boy named Atticus. He loved his life very much. He had the perfect house, the sweetest teachers, and the best friends!

Atticus's parents both worked for the military. They had lived all over the world! But not Atticus. He had always lived in the same house.

Then, one day, everything changed.
Atticus was playing with his dogs when he
heard his daddy shout, "It's official!"

Mommy began to jump up and down.
"PCS time, Florida here we come!"

Atticus watched, confused,
as his parents danced and laughed.

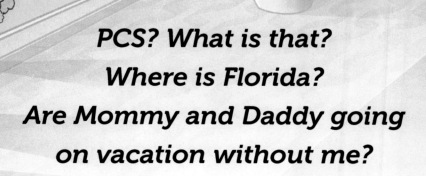

PCS? What is that?
Where is Florida?
Are Mommy and Daddy going
on vacation without me?

Mommy noticed him listening and picked him up.
"Great news, love," she said.
"We have a PCS to Florida coming up!"
"What's a PCS?" Atticus asked.

Mommy twirled him around. "It means we're moving to Florida. Think of it as a Positive Change of Scenery!"

"But . . . I don't want to leave," Atticus said,
his eyes beginning to water.
"I love my friends and teachers here.
How will they find me?"

Daddy handed him a cup of water.
"I promise, we will Provide Communication and Support!
PCS will be an adventure," he said.

Notify family and friends of the PCS. Pick which platforms you would like to utilize for communication. Exchange usernames, phone numbers, and e-mail addresses. Set dates on the calendar to look forward to.

"You know, at the new house you'll have your own room,"
Mommy told Atticus. "That means we have to
Prepare, Create, and Shop. PCS, your room will impress!"

"I don't have to share with Callista anymore?"
Atticus asked, looking at his baby sister.

"Nope!" Mommy said. "Even better, we can decorate your room any way you want!"

Atticus could hardly believe it.
Any way he wanted?
Maybe a jungle? No.
The ocean? No.
The sky, like where
Daddy worked! Yes!

Think of a theme for a bedroom. Look at what household items you can repurpose. Set them aside and mark them in a box. Begin working on small projects together to create excitement about the room.

The next morning, Atticus woke up to find the house filled with boxes. "Cool! A fort!" he shouted.

He scurried around collecting his toys to bring in with him.

At dinner, Daddy talked about the places they could visit on the drive to Florida.

"We need to Plan Cool Stops! PCS, where to next?"

Begin sorting and organizing items in the home. Boxes make cool forts and obstacle courses!

A few days later, Atticus's mom picked him up
from his last day of school.

When they got home, there was a huge truck outside.
Inside, he saw a few boxes. Everything else was gone!
Atticus couldn't believe how different the house looked!

"Well, that's it. The movers just left," Mommy said.
"Our things should be in Florida soon, just like us.
But tonight . . . we camp!"

Daddy lifted Atticus onto his shoulders
and took him to his perfect backyard.
Outside there were tents and sleeping bags.

"Tonight will be fun!" Daddy said.
"Pizza, Camping, and S'mores. PCS, oh yes!"

PARENT'S MOVING TIP

*Make your last night in the old house fun.
Set up tents, sleeping bags, and s'mores
in the backyard or living room.*

Atticus woke up in the car.
Baby Callista was next to him, still asleep in her car seat.

"Pssst. Atticus, wake up," Daddy whispered.
"We're at the beach!"

Atticus wiped his eyes until he felt more awake.
The sun was just coming up over the vast, beautiful ocean.
While Mommy stayed with Callista, he and Daddy made
sandcastles, splashed in the water, and collected seashells.

"I think I am going to like Florida," Atticus said.
"Playing, Castles, and Seashells, PCS is the best!"

PARENT'S MOVING TIP

Plan stops to break up your trip and
help the kids release some energy.

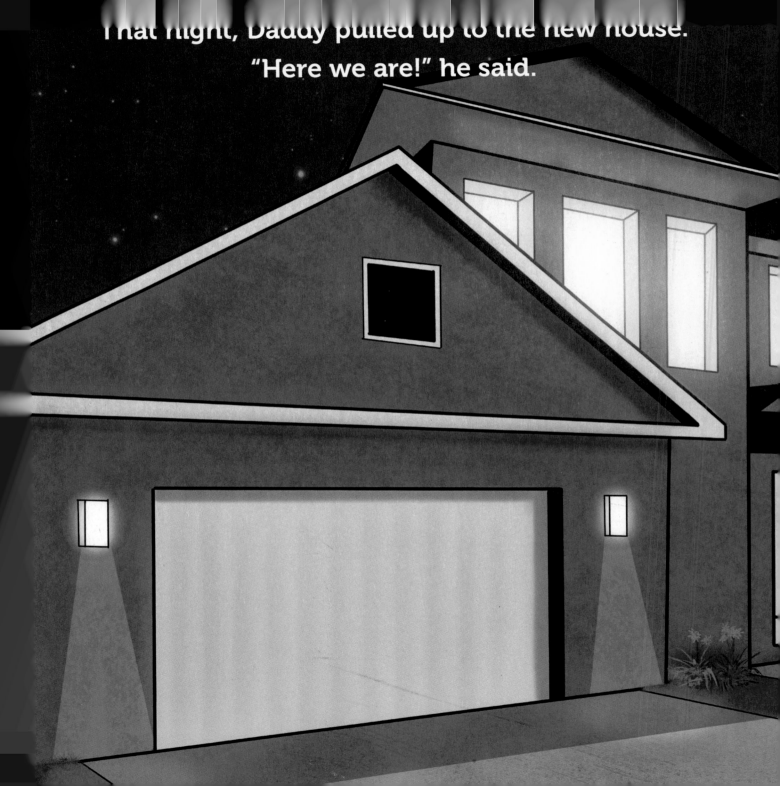

That night, Daddy pulled up to the new house.
"Here we are!" he said.

Atticus waited nervously to be unbuckled, and then hopped out of the car. He slowly walked around his new house. It looked nice.
Maybe this wouldn't be so bad, after all!

The next day, Daddy took Atticus and Callista to the park. When they got home, Atticus saw the moving truck in the driveway. Inside, his brand-new room was being put together with all of his favorite belongings.

Now this feels like home!
Perfect, Comfortable, and Special.
"Atticus," Mommy said with a laugh,
"this PCS is making the house a mess!"

A few days later,
Mommy brought Atticus to his new school.

"Here we are," she said. "Now remember
PCS—Polite, Courageous, Smile."

Atticus shook his head and clung to her leg.
Mommy gave him a hug. "You'll be fine. I promise."

Slowly, Atticus made his way inside.
The other kids looked up. Then one little girl ran over.

"Hi! Do you want to play blocks with me?"
Atticus nodded shyly.

Then, with a last look at his mom, he followed the girl.

That afternoon, Atticus was laughing and dancing with his friends when the classroom door opened.

"Mommy!" he shouted, running over.
"My class is so fun, and I have so many new friends!
We Played, Colored, and Sang. PCS," he said.

Then Atticus frowned.
"Mommy, I don't want to move again.
Can we stay here for a while?"

Mommy kissed and hugged him.
"Yes, Atticus, welcome to your new home!"

Made in the USA
Middletown, DE
10 July 2021